I0553194

Tales of the Urban Shaman

Philosophy of Action, Design, and Multiplicity

Book 7

Dan Paul

ProAct 2525

Contents

Chapter 1
Land of the Lost

The cliff was hidden. The path was disappearing. The tree tops that used to tower over her head were level with her knees. The catastrophic danger was a few feet away. Slowly, she inched forward. The tree tops and flora were dense; the ground was vanishing. They were hiking for a day and a half. She was separated from the other two. It was late afternoon, and it had been 20 minutes since she last saw the others. The path disappeared. She had little experience hiking in these areas. With the ground vanishing and no path, it was time to decide. How could she find the others? If she kept going, she could fall off the cliff, and, with help days away, she could easily not make it. The decision became apparent; she had to return and find the trail. At this point, it was the only logical choice, but the path had vanished, so it was challenging to find where to go. Without a compass or landmarks, she was lost. Like other challenges, she took a deep breath and entered her mind to find the right direction. The path needed to be clarified. The goal showed itself, and after careful consideration and an eye for what would undermine the process and the goals, she decided what must be done.

She tried to sleep, but it kept nagging her endlessly; why would someone do that? The pain sent an electric shock jolting her spine, through the leg bones and zooming out the toes. It wasn't the first time, but that didn't remove the pain. She gave up and got up. Nothing would stop her, even death. She had it planned out. Exactly what would happen after she dies? Releasing bots could generate human existence through artificial intelligence. A calculation had to be finished in 5 months. She avoided it and could no longer not do it. Humans no longer have a chance. Without AI, humans can't compete with a human AI interface. AI is a quantum leap in intelligence that humans are not capable of. It's like trying to do the math of a calculator without a calculator. AI is to humans as humans are to dogs. Training for two lifetimes will not prepare you to calculate faster than a calculator. You will never equal a calculator. She refused the bots many times, but now it was either do or die fighting. Harangued by the idea, she began to do push-ups.

 With a break, she was on the dance floor. With no one else motivated, she jammed an abstract repertoire of improvisations. She lost herself in the music, the moment, and a forever fascination with sound driving the body into action. It was another unknown yet familiar trance of the body, leaving traces of energy, action, and transformation. She felt like a wanderer through seconds, a path of time, a stream of energy in action. All this flows from person to plant, to animal, to person, to rock, to talk, to an abstract awareness that brings dreams into reality.

The sun twinkled through the branches. In a sleepy moment, she fell into a haze. She had to leave Los Angeles. The urban decay wore down her energy and frazzled her nerves. The chaos of the past took her out of the forest. They were living on the edge of Skid Row. Somehow the area was plagued with drug addicts, hookers, endless traffic, noise, and clamor from those who used the place to shoot drugs and party. A group of squatters and anarchists took the building after the city boarded it up. They began fixing it, building a fence, and setting up a ten-year operation to construct another reality. They were building an infoshop, a place for people to meet their needs without selling their time for money to the dominant machine. A court order was on the front door. They had five days to get out. Typically, this meant that they would have to prepare for battle or leave until the city had changed the locks, boarded up the place, and come back and retake it. Some Earth First activists were on their way from the mountains. With life facing another tailspin, she rolled the dice and rode to the mountains. A breeze blew open the canopy, and suddenly, she was back in the forest.

Going backward, an opening appeared. She had to find the path, but where? She had to find the others or face the wild alone. With little experience, she had yet to learn of the dangers. Without a tent, she would be exposed to all those creatures who thrive at night. She took a deep breath. It's all a process. Take one step, then the next, and so on till it's finished, but what was the next step? She put a marker on the ground to orient her position. She walked in one direction, set a marker, walked another 25 steps, and set another marker. She charted three directions and laid out paths in those directions. One direction led to the cliff, so she didn't check in that direction. Somehow, she would find the path. It had to happen. Mapping out the area she was in could orient her to find the path. It was unclear, but it was the best option she could think of. She would meet her friends again; it was a matter of time, but what if it didn't work? She'd be stranded in the mountains, the time would crawl, and fears would magnify; anxiety was at the door, but she had faced struggles in the past, and the process was the same. Go with the process. Avoid fears.

With water running low, keeping her mind in check was a top priority. Dehydration reduces your ability to think and act logically. She had to focus. Time was running out. Her friends, Where were they? She kept walking, not thinking of looking back. The slow pace of the others was too much for her. Now, it was too late to slow down. She looked over the marker and the three paths she outlined. It had to work, but it wasn't working. With a focus on her core energy, she continued. With branches and flowers, she marked her trails. With no other choice, she focused on her path. They were out there. She started hiking on the last path. Confusion was approaching as hunger set in. Perhaps she could eat some of the plants, but she didn't want to risk getting poisoned. If she could avoid losing her mind, she'd be able to find a way out. She traced her steps backward, and as she looked around, she noticed something that could be a path. She set a marker where she turned off her path. Keeping her bearings was important. If she saw moss on the side of a tree, that would indicate north. She found the path but needed to be aware of the direction. They were in the middle of the hike. She wanted to go forward and tried to understand the right way.

No one had been on the path while they were walking. It was an uncommon route that appeared and disappeared as the energy of the jungle swallowed it up. She could feel something coming on. It was a growth spurt. She lost her core in the chaos and confusion of the heat, lost in the jungle. The swirling energy jammed her balance. Now, on the path, things were changing. A tingle in her deepest senses began to light up. She embraced the earth, air, land, fire, and the sky. Something was happening, and she couldn't name it. That was alright; her energy rose like sunshine after the rain. The tingle turned into spurts; perhaps the energy of the fingerprints of Siberian ginseng and a dash of weed gave power to the pulse, and now another clarity came upon her. She saw traces of their footprints at the lowest level of the forest. Ponderosa pine, giant boulders, and brush were very hot and dry. The path was 3 feet wide and well-traveled at some points. Midway through the first day, they came upon a small store where, of course, they had Coca-Cola. Off and on, and back and forth, the time would spin its forecast for something beyond this quiet platitude of a remote existence, a place that forever was inhospitable to most humans.

The path began to fade. Time dragged on as if forever. The other two had to be close. The question kept burning: what will happen? Could she lose the path and not get back? It's happened to other people. It could be impossible to avoid. Such is the case when you are so far from anyone that predicting what could happen is beyond a stretch. With a whisper of light, the birds appeared. The ecosystem was loaded with insects, which supported a long food chain that included humans. In and out of the blue sky were ravens singing a dark chorus of another future. She backtracked to her markers. It was the security she could behold. The path picked up coherence and led to a river. The current was strong, and the water was nearly waist-high. It would be a risky challenge to cross. She looked for other options. The path picked up on the other side of the river. Perhaps they crossed in the dry season or after the surge of flood waters subsided. With a gusty wind, the clouds rolled in. The change in the light generated copious differences. Almost like a light switch, patterns vanished. Nearly blinded by the light, she took refuge in the shade.

As the night approached, she became uneasy and started planning camp. She was hoping something would happen to allow her to forego the decision. Could she make a shelter? Perhaps, but What if the leaves were poisonous? What if there were insects in the trees or an animal using the tree? After all, who would want some invader to take over their habitat, housing, and means of living? That would be a territorial use of the tree. The questions nagged her as her hopes for finding the others faded. How could she lose them in the first place? The closer she got, the farther away she felt. In a few moments, things could be completely different. Was she going in the right direction? Things looked new, and as far as she knew, the path was still going up the mountain. Chances were good that she would come across something telling her she was at the top.

Tangled in the wild, a sound stirred her into LA. Her brigade was going to set up an info-shop at 341. With two others, they wanted to expand and make a base for the community to build a better life outside the mainstream. This required an uncommon discipline, which is typically the opposite of what people think of when they hear about punks and anarchists, but it makes results. She had to get back in action. Keeping a focus over the long term is what generates the most desirable results. Though setting up housing, healthcare, and food for those in need was draining, seeing people take small steps to make a life worth living grew her motivation. Somehow, they would keep the building and fight the police or take it back after they leave.

The flowers adorned a deep purple. Suddenly, she was back in the forest. The pedals enveloped her mind with a scent of another world. The energy of the wild danced a jiggle of happy, go sad, then keep moving. She took the purple light in like food. With deep breaths, she spread the plants through her body. She became purple and let it meander a passion of the something not yet. Connecting with the plant world opened another channel into the beyond, something to give her the elements to keep going. In the sparse light and tender moments, she opened a secret world.

Chapter 2
Phantoms of Life and Love

The Path of Logic and Counterlogic

The silence broke. The light hit the walls and dispersed a canopy of another awareness. In the background, the traffic broke the silence. She kept wondering how she got on this path. Why didn't she fit in like the others? Looking through the past, in the hazy noise, a memory took hold. She was at a religious gathering. The priest was talking. Over and over, she thought, "Wow, this doesn't make any sense." The logic was false, and who wants another authority? After all, how many times did she read about the abuse of young people by priests? Does zero not equal zero in a house of worship? So much of it was capricious and arbitrary. The seeds of rebellion started there and continued through a rocky path beyond boundaries.

Worms and Gophers

It was a cool morning in the spring. As the forever ice and snow began to melt, another reality emerged. The solid ground became muddy, then dry and muddy, and eventually home to new life. She kept digging around, looking. They were putting a fence up—another barrier to stop people, plants, and animals from circulating. The lines destroyed continuity and the flow. Somewhere, there had to be something else. Who needs all these fences that make blocks of boredom and complacency? Life was coming out of the frozen mud. Eventually, night crawlers, worms, and bugs would show themselves. All of that rapidly disappeared with each house, driveway, and endless grass. The grass had to be mowed and mowed and mowed. The grasshoppers were gone, with no crickets, gophers, or anything. They clear-cut the forest and clear-cut the grass. There's nothing to play with or look at. All the grass looks the same. The weeds gave difference, something to look at, touch, taste, and explore. All of that was going down a sinkhole called development. Everything to connect to was eliminated. Looking around, she could find a stack of wood, turn it over, and look under it. Perhaps something would come out.

The authoritarian black hole.

She wanted to act but couldn't. What was stopping her? Something, but she didn't know what it was. The struggle continued, but there was nothing to push against. Was it in her mind, or was it language? Perhaps it was other. Like what? She fell back into a haze. The ideas came and left. How could this something be stopping her? If only she could be like the others who weren't riddled with self-doubt, constantly questioning every step they made. How could all these other people be comfortable with their direction? For her, it was like stepping on a slippery floor, quicksand, and, some days, like thin ice. It started in the stomach and circulated. It was nausea with sparks and streaks of lighting-like pain. Don't other people question why they are doing what they do? The train rolled on, and she fell into a half-sleep. The teachers drove her up the wall. The religion, nationalism, and culture of the country were imposed upon her. There was never a choice, and how was she to know what was true or false? At an early age, the logical fallacies of religion kept nagging at her. Why did she have to learn all the dictates of faith when it had no logical integrity? The endless mountains of orders and false statements tangled a dark web of inconsistencies that prevented her from taking action. She couldn't make decisions but didn't know why.

Squat Life

Far from communication, she could only imagine what the others were going through. Living in the squat was a forever challenge. It was hard to know what would come next. The police, fire department, building inspectors, or someone trying to take over a spot, some addicted to drugs, others for housing. As soon as a room, or even a spot, would open, somebody would claim it, move in as fast as possible, and then guard it from others. When people don't communicate and abide by basic ideas of human decency, it can undermine the squat and generate endless conflicts. You don't go into other people's space without asking, leave a mess in the hallway, or do things that compromise the safety of people in the building. Without some basic ideas like this, the squat would crumble from internal conflicts or police violence. She had been through it more than a few times and wasn't afraid, but she didn't want another battle with the police.

Flashing Oblique

She was not prepared for what was about to happen. Lost in the intensity of the forest, she fell away from the matters of the physical world and put her mind in relaxed mode. In a few moments, all of that faded away as the world flashed by, the seconds rolling, the images fading, in the soft, rolling, fluffy clouds exposing the blond hair and blue eyes in the sky. A cute whisper gave way to a cracking thunder, an unwise cracking the bliss, feigning smashing atoms and releasing energy. In a few slow seconds, another wish faded and passed as an oblique reference stranded in the last temptation, the final humiliation, the lost harangue, an abstract chronicle of referents to another beyond.

Smother Slang

The birds began to smother her. They were fluffy, soft, laughing, and smothering. All oxygen vanished as the vacuum of dense matter internalized the space. A scent enveloped her mind. She reached for the stratosphere as another dimension became apparent. She lifted the world into a forever zone on a fast track to nowhere. Everything became soft, warm, and fuzzy as an abstract dance took her on a path, second after second, and the light opened a breeze. She began to choke and struggle to breathe. It was all so difficult to imagine or comprehend.

In fleeting moments, a dawn arose. She felt the energy. More and more, it took her over. She parked her bike and moved to meet the others. Still, even while talking, she could feel it move her. They met the night before. Something magical happened. Something was happening. It felt warm and smooth, tender and soft, and something else, something kept drawing her in. It was never like this. Impossible to describe, she struggled to find a connection. The energy was potent. She thought of nothing else day and night. A dream opened up like a feather of light moving through the sky. She realized it was all about connecting to what sustains us. The leaves twinkled a new dawn.

Was it day or night, reality or illusion? All was scrambled but impossible to decipher. She put it all together and tried to organize it, but it fell apart, dissolved, and vanished. Cloudy illusions tampered with the real. With too much effort, she moved. How could it happen this way? The bugs fluttered, stopped, and whirled around. Was she awake or asleep, on Earth or stuck in space again? The abduction started again. It was impossible to know how, why, or when they happened. The walls began to move. With a gesture, she worked on pulling it together. The tiny moments got lost in another trial. Spinning motions told another story. How long would it last? The emergency was extended for another two months. At best, things looked like a war zone sprinkled with these odd entities, which combined elements of plants, animals, humans, and machines. A few came out of the ground.

Some floated in the air, and others were attached to anything else. The genetic difference was arrested in the last flash— things combined and split in altered ways. Plants were growing out of a chair with human legs on the bottom, a giant eye in the middle, and magnolia flowers spewing out the top. The glue of reality spun out of awareness. The categories of time and space warped into illusion. Nothing happened in a fast or slow way. With a toned and antic presence, another wave channeled the beyond into nowhere.

She opened a tiny morsel of the abstract and jumped on the forever wheel.

Forever Wheel

In moments of tremble and fascination, she grabbed a button to hold on tight and gripped the air with all the energy available. Moments stretched on for days. It was like being in a desert without sunshine or heat. Reality was stuck. The bunny cat began to whisper and tell a story. It was the size of a small ship. Warm, fuzzy, and delightful trails of entities opened a line of simulation. The pure fantasy of it all turned into a beyond of twilight and soft fingers.

Failure to Emanate

She pushed the emanate button, and it didn't work. That thing was inside her, and this should work, but now it's becoming too late. She put in a new power pack. Still no response. Pump, ejaculate, and hit the kill button. The manual method was not supported.

Chronicles of Imaginations

Past the dock, a long line of people were walking on water. The levitator shoes held up well, but when they hit a fool pool, they would disintegrate, and then it was time to swim; if the water didn't vanish at flash point, they would crash to the bottom. It didn't happen often, and getting someone out of the deep hole was nearly impossible. She let the others walk on the wild side. After too many rescue attempts, she was tired of the same stories. Her parents were drug addicts who threw garbage out the window, let their apartment deteriorate, and rarely tended to her needs. Every couple of days, some emergency happened. It was a nuisance house.

People would do anything to get attention and then laugh at you. It was a debilitating place to be where bullying was common, and people blamed each other for something without answers.

Cupids Laser

She opened the heart of gold. In the quest for the magic moment, she noticed the clouds opening up; the sun shone a burst of light. She approached the man on the platform to find out which way the wind was blowing. A sweet and toxic smell triggered a memory that interrupted her motion. The days were long, the work was dull, and the pay was low. She could only think about quitting but was stuck. Like an indentured servant, she was caught in economic quicksand. Just using a car took one-third of her income, and for what? It kept breaking down. It was an endless source of anxiety. What if it broke down when she had to get to work? Or when it was cold and no one was around, or when she had no money to get it fixed, or what if the cops noticed some little thing wrong and pulled her over and destroyed her future? She had no interest in a fancy car, house, or apartment. She wanted a decent life with time to pursue what her life's energy led her to.

The day she quit was etched in her memory. It was a clear, cold day. People warned her that the pipes could freeze. She turned the faucet to drip to prevent freezing. The boss reprimanded her for that and other things unrelated to her. She tried to explain, but he kept interrupting her. The week before, she found another place to work. After negotiating the problem, he reprimanded her, so she told him to find someone else to do the work.

The moon opened her awareness. With a gentle toss, she fluffed her hair, grabbed her instrument, and flew off on her bicycle. Her force came from within and depended on her relations with the elements. She had to connect, feel the energy, and embrace the sky and the moon. In movement, she thrived. She could feel another presence in the light of the moon. The river was a quick ride. She found a spot on the rocks overlooking the valley on one side and took a long look to feed her imagination.

The rocks were alive. It was as clear as the mountain air. How people could not realize it was beyond her. She felt the energy, the connection, and the momentum. Now, it could be nothing else but a smooth space, alive, pulsing, emanating energy. How could that not be alive? The clouds began to clutter the sky. She felt like moving but knew she had to stay longer. The Earth, water, and sky were one, together forever, dancing on this path beyond the next second. She opened the bag and took a bite of the apple. Crispy, tart, and juicy, it invigorated her and opened another area to explore. The path, second after second, was hers and no one else's. She embraced the seconds and moments, the pain, the pleasure in abstraction, the long moments when all life seemed to disappear.

She ended the distractions. Putting her full force into movement was the beginning of another dance on the path. She wrote the list and spoke about it. Questions came to mind, and she spoke and wrote the answers, then spoke and wrote again. After short meditations, she jumped rope and went back at it again. In this process, she could make a solid direction. After she started, she didn't want any more questions to prevent her from moving on to the next step.

Nothing could stop her. She had to do it. She could consult others, but that may have to wait. The past revealed her mistakes, and the consequences made her remember what to avoid. She did another round of questions and answers and the goal. She whittled down the distractions, what to avoid, what to embrace, and fused the goal deep inside. Over and over, she tried to figure out what could go wrong and how to prevent what could stop what she was doing.

A group met. It was a casual event with a motley bunch from around the country. They hadn't seen each other for years and had been through more than too much. The crackdown started after a major offensive to gain housing, improve the food supply, and secure healthcare in the era of the impossible. The fascists gained power after they poisoned the water supply and blamed it on the opposition.

Chapter 3

Expressions of
the Magna Carta

In a tense moment, the hour turned green. No one had seen time in color. Green, red, yellow, or blue time—could this be another illusion of reality? Even the sophists would not question this. In a moment of fantastic time, it turned color.

The moments they had lived to fear were approaching. Many couldn't believe it would happen, thought it had to happen, and were shocked that it did happen. A fascist took power after a series of power grabs that baffled most. They were having their way after a series of events led the government to dissolve itself, and, in the resulting vacuum, a group of ultra-right-wing extremists seized power. Their goal was to end the liberal agenda once and for all. They controlled the most prominent industries and restricted economic advantage to the most loyal people. People who didn't conform to the ideal were put in work camps. With no respect for justice, they worked people until they could move no more. People were a tool to advance power. Any person who questioned the direction or purpose of work was put into a camp. The camps were being set up in many places. Some thought that the fasbots could make it work, but others knew that such a system could never sustain itself. A few people at the top did well, while the others obeyed orders, hoping the dictator would not give orders to take them away.

In a trance accident, like a human cicada, she came alive. Too often, it was the other way around. This time was another chance to see what it is. She turned the screw to just below flush, adjusted her glasses, and in her mind, she thought, "Why wait? Why hesitate, don't wait for too late," so said the procrastinator. She quickly muscled her way through after doing the push-ups, pilates, and stair climbing. Her core grew solid. Along the way is another tower. It's one you will never forget. So eyes on forever, and so will be your climb.

As the sun sets, another day rises. She kept reading in between thoughts and writing. Her mind gobbled a treasure of literature every month. Some say she could read ten pages per minute. So this other world became a watershed of the wild and the wonderful on the way to forever. So were the words of this other one, not a cyborg, and not a cicada, and not a human, precisely something else, something, an entity, perhaps an organism machine, a creature that "hath not existed, " which became the point. They had to fight back. The Trump takeover had the support of the Senate, which depended on big money from oil and products that exploit human weakness and addiction. Anyone who didn't fit the mold of a "good American" could be beaten up, thrown in prison, and killed. Now, their housing was under attack.

She took a break from the intensity of it all and walked outside. Dense vegetation greeted her. Over the years, their efforts paid off, as they learned to use wild and medicinal plants to help them get an edge over the opposition. Dandelion, burdock, Queen Anne's lace, and other plants helped her get through the hard times on the front line. She began drinking a mix of plants that grew well and were nutritious but unpleasant to eat fresh or cook with. Her clever idea was to extract the nutrition without using any energy and drink the cold brew to invigorate her body and expand awareness. Without money and a job, she could empower herself to live well outside the dominant codes. All day long, she saw people who could barely walk because they were addicted to food, drugs, and the poison of endless TV.

She met her friends in the park. They were on a hike through some rough areas of the city. They knew some people, and they were not so friendly. For years, the economy was on a downward trend. The vast storms knocked down trees, destroyed houses, and undermined the infrastructure that sustained their lives. It was a war zone without a war. Somehow, they kept going. Where else could they go? They were told the river would rise again and the floods would come. Having lived in the same place for many years, they couldn't imagine living anywhere else. The storm lasted three days, and a second goes by like a year. It was twice the size of the US, with a tornado core 100 miles in diameter. It was pulverizing 100 miles of vegetation and buildings per second. Trash and debris were everywhere. The bodies of people and animals were ground up and strewn about in all directions. The buildings shook, glass broke, and the power went out shortly after the storm began. People were getting used to it. They had no choice. Some left, but most could not get beyond the city's edge without saying goodbye forever. It was the last of New York City after the storm wiped Manhattan off the map.

Something vanished. The loudspeakers came on again. The unending propaganda left no room to think, remember, reflect, or imagine anything else. Yes, life would come and go, but another reality emerged. There used to be stores where you could buy anything you could imagine. Now, a bleak array of what survived the storms, the looting, the fascists, and the endless struggle for a working society where you could get what you want from the store and use it as you like.

It happened again. It was like cancer; even if you smash it down, it comes back again. The internal struggles never seem to stop. Many kept with it, even with all the problems. It may be the vision, the work, the people, the place, or something. It is now; somehow, she had to deal with the problem. She put on her boots and took moments to breathe and enjoy the beauty surrounding her. After the day starts, it goes by like a flash. The meetings went on and on and didn't go anywhere. The power struggles never seemed to stop. Mark broke into the building years ago and got the squat going. Eventually, he invited others to join. There were some rules in place, but now Mark wanted too much. He occupied three apartments out of ten. Two apartments were filled with junk and other building supplies. The 3rd one he used for himself and two dogs, who were another issue. He commanded people around and acted like no one else was doing the important work that needed to be done. Of course, many of the opposite ideas were true. The group had been meeting for years. They invited Mark to join, but he refused.

Some had lived in functioning collectives before. In a couple of years, they figured out how to do it democratically. They had been through the strong leader cancer before. They had weekly meetings. Any member could contribute an item to the agenda. They specified whether it was a topic for discussion or to make a decision and how much time they wanted to discuss the issue. The meetings were the core entity that kept the coop functioning. Decisions were made about how to own, manage, and maintain the buildings they lived in. They developed a work job system to complete the work and keep the buildings. People could live in the collective for a year and leave. The coop would still function when 1 or 2 people left. The whole thing was a process. Yes, a strong leader may be able to take over the collective, but only if people let it happen.

How does the project, like a squat, coop, or media project, start? Sometimes, strong-minded people take action when no one else will. They put their lives on the line to make something happen. They do things no one else will do. They are committed and take action to make sure the project happens. They can be counted on to get the job done. They take the lead when no one else will. When they do so, they think about the big project and what they will get from it. Some want community, others wish to respect, and some want to make it their particular project and put their name on it. Often, a coop or squat will have these divergent perspectives. This creates tensions. People want fairness and to know they will get what they put in. So, if you have a strong leader, which is often necessary to get a project started, the strong leader will want to get more out of the project than someone who comes later, sweeps the floors, and does the dishes.

Democratic coops have solutions for this. People make decisions at a weekly meeting. Everyone who is a member is supposed to come to the meeting. If you don't come and later object to what is going on, people may ask, "Why didn't you come to the meeting?" Remember that when people come to meetings, they stop what they are doing to advance the group's goals. It requires effort to go to a meeting and make decisions. She never totally understood how people became so brainwashed, but then she thought of the amount of time people are glued to media that directs them into production and consumption. If they borrow money from people to consume, they will become like indentured servants who can never pay back the debt they accumulate. From all directions, the paths led to the indentured servitude to the machine; some called it capitalism, some called it fascism; as the man whining on the screen to capture her attention annoyed her, she found a habit of getting her out of the pit.

She gazed out the window. They hopped on the train, and in a moment of blue sky and haze, she fell into a memory. Catholic school never left her. She wondered why she was not so talkative and what prevented her from feeling in the groove. That nagging thing kept popping up when she wanted to move ahead. Was it because she had no confidence? She was too young to have an idea of what was going on. They were working on English when the bell rang. It was a standard fire drill. She was in a small town, and the numbers kept clicking. Click, click, click, like the rim of a ten-speed bicycle when the wheels are new. When the bell rang, the kids began running out the door. The fear rose to a crescendo after the smoke appeared, and mayhem ensued.

Someone fell, then one and two and more. Suddenly, three kids were on top of her. What happened next was a blur. Pain blew open, and she struggled and was able to get out of the building. It was like sparks of shocks in her joints. Her face fell slump. Smoke came out the windows as the fire trucks arrived. How did the fire start? Who would do such a thing? Was it an accident? A prank, an attack? Or was someone on some campaign to disrupt rural life's everyday boredom and ritual? They waited for the trucks to leave. She began to wonder if they would call off school. The principal came up to her and told her to come with him. They went to an office in the Church next door. He began to ask her questions, and then she began to cry.

The phone was loud and in their ears. It talked about one person as many genders, a common idea in the community and unthinkable in the dominant society. In a silent moment, a spider woke up her imagination. An endless clutter of notices opened a way out of the dogma. The needle went in fast and clean. Not a peep was heard. She looked the other way. She was on the path. One second, then another. A path of time, you have to go through it to the next step. In a cloud of thunder, another awakening lit her mind on the horizon. The tree of heaven rose beyond comprehension. The shadow was as infinite as numbers. Quaking in blue thunder, her energy rose out and beyond. In another breath, a silent mayhem clouded the entrance. They were looking for who?

The scavenger hunt led down an alley and mysteriously into a surreal playground. The imagination became real as desire enveloped the energy of all involved. Happy antics floated in the twilight. The colors of five-dimensional disco balls scrambled the laws of physics, abstractions, and secret metaphors.

Like others, she intended to explore the oblique signals referred to by the anti-ists. A trembling secret left a gaping hole in the future. With destiny at stake, she opened a key to awareness. She was more than against AI, but now she could not wait. With an opening came a chance at the ultimate future. The references came and left too quickly for the slightest hesitation. In a slow moment, the colors of forever appeared and disappeared.

The endless battle with AI made all her other problems a picnic. It was challenging to know who or what was behind it. The attacks would be coordinated and debilitating. In the middle of the night, the phone would start ringing, the computers kept turning on, and something was ringing the doorbell. She tried to turn off the phone, computer, and radio, which was impossible. Even unplugging it would do nothing. After all the electronics turned on, noises from the doors and windows made it sound like something was trying to get in. Next, the water started running. The sense of a total loss of control enveloped her. She was dead tired and buried herself in bed. With earplugs, glasses, and warm clothes, she could ignore it and go back to sleep.

Chapter 4

Challenging the Dominant Codes

Her disgust with the dominant codes activated her. She advanced the means to meet needs sustainably. Having seen perfectly useable belongings hauled away with heavily polluting and dangerous trucks to a landfill, she was motivated to avoid the dead ends of production and consumption. Some talked of freedom, but that was an illusion as people were suckered into becoming indentured servants. Buried in debt to get an education, house, or endless credit card debt, people dug their graves as they spun the infinite treadmill of production, consumption, and debt. Watching capitalist media made them crave an expensive house, education, or belongings they didn't need. Others fell deep into debt when they were in an accident or fell sick and had colossal hospital bills. All of this could destroy the economy for generations. With collective action, they could advance their housing, culture, and work. They composted, ate vegetarian food, and used less energy. They were years ahead of the dominant codes, which pushed endless use of raw materials, fossil fuel use, and a dead-end lifestyle of infinite work, drudgery, and required subservience.

It was a fantastic day in the spring. They were on campus and set up for action. A war chest tour was in the works. The endless warfare that destroyed people, buildings, the means to live, and the environment had to stop. The war machine produces jobs building military equipment that may be used against people in an unjust and immoral way. Bullying people with warfare and economic terror was a foreign policy loaded with land mines. It might not happen next week or the week after, but it could tear down a good part of the country when it comes. Without borders on nations that could dominate the country and without any severe other competition, the killing of innocent people went on and on. Also, with the killings came the destruction of the means to live. Farming, processing, and distribution of goods were undermined and destroyed in many areas. Yes, people could adapt, but the weapons produce toxins that spread to people through the air, land, water, plants, and animals. Bombs made with depleted uranium generate hideous congenital disabilities in children and discourage people from having children. With a close eye on the future, they could not let this go. In the US, many lived a high standard of living, but the war front was another story. Who would sit by as more and more of the country's resources destroyed other people and countries? But too soon, the moments faded into another zone.

The crash blasted the window into shreds. It was obvious who it was. It was a two-bell alarm. It was either a broken code or a warning. Then boom, another hit the side of the wall, and more were coming. They went into battle formation. One person on each floor had their defensive and offensive means to win. With a stack of bricks on the roof, they began an offensive. The bricks went flying against the mob, which quickly dispersed. Still, the damage had been done, and who knew when they would return. They were happy to have the dogs around to alert them and be on the front lines when the invaders came to attack.

They used theory to define and advance action. In daily sessions, they listed topics for discussion, proposals, and decisions to make. With group thinking, they went beyond the common assumptions and tendencies to advance a sustainable philosophy of action. Most thought nothing of using whatever resources they wanted, which was the problem. It was common for someone to buy a piece of land, cut the trees, and put up a house. This killed and injured insects, rodents, birds, and animals and made them homeless. Years later, many plants and animals would no longer be around. Quickly, the frogs disappeared, and the salamanders and birds could not make it anymore. With minds of action, they were involved in and connected to the living world. With the skills they nurtured, they made their housing, food, and means to live.

With sweat and drive, they learned to keep their housing in good condition. They fixed and set up housing to meet needs sustainably in the community. The days seemed long, but the motivation was strong. They learned to divide the work so people learned skills and connected to their work and their place. Every 4th person was on maintenance. One took care of the outside, another the common areas, and the other took care of the kitchen and bathroom. You could work on various projects to manage, clean, and operate a building with numerous bedrooms. People shared a bathroom, kitchen, laundry, work room, and various amenities as determined by the many. With regular meetings, they could take advantage of the group's variety of intelligences. One person was good at finance, cooking, cleaning, and maintenance.

The culture of the collective was laid back. You could invite a friend for dinner, or people from other collectives could enjoy a meal together. All food was organic, vegetarian, or vegan. Some coops have one person who makes deserts, granola, and bread. Our coop had large amounts of organic food to provide for 20 people. Meals were served 3-6 nights per week. You could order a plate for later, eat inside or outside, and enjoy daily news at the dinner table. Giant pots of soup, bowls of bread, and salad nourish and invigorate the collectives. Dinners provide ample space to plan, organize, share, distribute, and work on projects. For parties, the benches were loaded with members. Honor Among Thieves would play, and the place would rumble.

A group specialized in housing. They learned how to buy man, age, and operate the buildings they lived in. They did it collectively without authoritarian leaders, generating strength and power in the members. All the essential activities that had to be done were put on a list. Each item on the list was put into a work job system. Some jobs were mostly manual labor, and others focused on running the books, maintaining the building, and organizing the activities to keep the operation going. People rotated jobs, so for four months, you would learn to fix the building, for the next, how to do the books, and the next time, make dinner for all. As you rotated doing different jobs, you gained the skills to secure housing without a landlord or anyone.

The oppression of gender roles stifled the desire of many, and for what? Patriarchy was dead. Non-privilege people wanted it gone. Aren't we all a part of this world regardless of how we comport ourselves? Why should someone have to conform to an erratic, undefined set of codes that define what a "man" should do and what a "woman" should do? She opened the blinders and let the light in. Many had given up or ignored the codes for years. Gender was fluid in the squat. You could dress or act as you like as long as you didn't push it on others. Yes, people may not like what you are doing; yes, you may have people support you through times of oppression; and yes, if you are a guy or not, you should be able to wear what you like.

In the social culture, the potential to learn other ways of interpreting events can occur. Through dinner conversations, informal discussions, and meetings, members develop an awareness of another way to empower themselves: owning, operating, and managing their buildings. Most have never conducted themselves in a social context in which their opinion mattered. The decisions made at a meeting have direct and immediate consequences for the members. If someone doesn't do the work they said they would, problems can accrue, and members must figure out how to deal with it or live with the consequences. As members figure out how to make decisions about crucial matters, their confidence grows, and they can solve whatever problems arise. Their skills grow and secure the building and members' housing for the future. The coop becomes more secure as members go through all the work jobs and learn the fundamentals. With more than one member able to do the essential jobs, another can quickly take over if one member can't. A large-scale work job system could make it easy for one member to join another coop and make it easy for a person to move from one coop to another. The social element will determine if it will work. They have discussions and meetings and make decisions.

In the cooperative, people have secure housing. They don't have to worry about getting evicted when the rent goes up, or the landlord wants to use the building for other purposes. People who live in the building control the building and determine how to pay the bills, whether they can make a garden or workroom in the basement, or whether to have a benefit for those in need. With secure housing, people can focus on social projects, and because of the low rent, some may be able to travel for more extended periods with less worry about how the rent will be paid. Because Coops maximize the benefits of sweat equity, they can provide quality housing for 30-50% less than market-rate housing. Because coops require less money for housing, people have more freedom to do what they want. They don't have to work day and night for housing, only to worry about when the landlord wants their apartment back.

Of course, the coops are not without their disadvantages. Nearly all Americans are programmed to think as an individual. They can't imagine how a group can function. Most can only think of what they can get out of the coop. Other methods advance the group and take the individuals beyond what they could do on their own by using a process that taps into the powers of everyone living there. This group mind may be less swayed by the personal interests of those who can't think in terms of what is in the interest of everyone. Decisions are made based on how the group would benefit more than one member using the coop to benefit themselves.

Coops may offer a buffer against Artificial Intelligence. How could that work? If you can meet needs without AI, can it be avoided? Perhaps some of it. When people own and manage their buildings, they have more control and more ability to keep the housing for a long time. No human entity will likely outperform AI. If AI runs all the other housing, non-AI housing will likely not perform as well. That depends on many things. If my job is to clean the bathroom, can I raise the money to buy a robot to do it or pay for it myself and have the robot do the job? I could have the bathroom job for an extended time, and the robot does my job. Eventually, people may lose the skills required to clean the bathroom.

Coops provide quality, low-income, sustainable housing to their members to advance a life worth living. As members have lower rent and food bills each month, they are required to work less. The capitalist economy takes their power to do what they want. With market-rate housing, many people need help paying their bills. They work many hours and have no energy when they come home. They must rest, recover, and prepare for work the next day. In a cooperative, members pay less rent and can afford housing, food, and expenses with a part-time or low-income job. This means they can keep their low-income job and still be able to afford decent housing and have time to do what they want.

The fascists used any means to undermine the value and practical functions of the cooperatives. In the media, they cut down on the value and accomplishments of the cooperatives. At a certain point, the right felt downtrodden and responded violently. They destroyed any symbols of the achievements of the social era. They attacked, injured, and killed key members of those who pushed for freedom, democracy, and the free expression of those who challenge the code. People who dress or act, play, build, invent, pray, or worship differently will be eliminated subdued or enslaved to advance the goals of the fascists. Many will be beaten up and injured, and some will not make it. Others will leave before it's too late, live elsewhere, or return if things turn around.

Chapter 5
Bot Idioms

To the untrained eye, they appeared to be like cicadas flying around without order or direction. The bots were on the move. All was quite the opposite. It's like someone being ultra-efficient in the work area. They work on 3-5 goals with multiple do-lists stacked across time and space. One set of tasks was for a project to be completed in 3 hours, another five days, and others years later. Many of the bots were made by other bots. Eventually, a typical machine language evolved as humans programmed intelligence to create intelligence. Some called it stacking language. For most people, the boredom and monotony of the activity were enticing for only the most autistic person—someone who could endlessly focus on the smallest detail and had no interest in conversation.

For some time, humans have been losing control of technology. The more they relied on machines to make things, the less skill and intelligence they generated. Or was it the opposite? The whole process was so huge with so much momentum that it was difficult to imagine how it could stop. Some say a solar storm or electromagnetic pulse could knock out the internet, and everything would come to a grinding stop. Others said global warming would extinguish people, which would stop the bots, but could bots or humbots keep going on earth if the conditions for human life did not exist? The next progression of evolution is for humans to become half robots and then total bots, potentially living forever and being the last round of evolution. Since bots don't need food, they are more sustainable. Also, people never had the chance to become eternal. Why not download your brain and put it in something not riddled with pain and too many unknowns? People can't live when the low temperature is 105 degrees. With many areas of the earth too hot to live, humbots evolved and were designed to exist in hotter temperatures.

Keeping the building and repair shops open was a high priority for the botniks, who were the most machine-like and had the highest status in the rank of humans, humbots, and botniks. Some had systems that replaced systems of the body. For years, it was possible to get replacement organs with a life expectancy of 50 years. Some were grown in containers, and others were made with bots. You could opt to be a machine or a living entity. Most people were both.

Predictions indicated that botniks would take over the whole world in 73.5 years. The calculations were available at any place at any time. Bot fuel is typically math, science, and engineering. What most humans hated, the bots loved, which allowed them to take over the world. They did the most hated and tedious jobs. Bots could live anywhere and do anything, but they had no motivation. This was the missing component from all bots. The top priority of the decade was to make motivation. It was illegal, so they did it in bunkers, mostly in space or deep underground. Space bots and under-bots worked on this the most. Of course, they were specially designed for that purpose.

With all this activity going on, it was only a matter of time before there would be conflict. It took a lot of work to tell what a bot was up to. Many would never challenge what was happening. A lot of the conflict was about the interface. How could a human communicate with a humbot or a botnik? Some areas had an interface, but often entities got stuck. A log jam would ensue. First, a human and botnik would get stuck, and others eventually wanted in on the same materials, equipment, or information or to get the attention or services from another entity. So they would be link stuck. Stickiness was a big problem. Some places were called Stuck Land or Stuckville, and one was called Stuckopolis. Why would someone want to go to one of these places? The logic was, like most of these areas, counter-logical. Most were stuck in counterlogic.

Counterlogic How did counterlogic function? The notion of function was not counter-logical, so the term was riddled with contradiction. After all, how do you resolve something that generates endless contradictions? Counterlogic was related to dysfunction, which implied an abstract level of mayhem in the system. Also, counter logic generated endless questions. Each question had to be resolved before moving to the next level. Fixation, counter fixation, and counter function generated more questions than answers. At the level of counter-abstraction, the functions went into abstract rewind. In the gobbled mess of counterlogic, no extensions were permitted or erased.

In an **abstract trance,** there was no choice but to let go. She took a sip of tea and looked for the others. The bot world would have to wait for another signal, another set of changes and challenges. She glided, swooned, and landed. A major storm was coming. Storms used to last for days, but now they are weeks long, and many people do not make it. Humans were put to the test. Humbots could make it through quickly, and botniks would expand during the storms. Humans and humbots couldn't work during the storms. Some began to wonder if the botniks were making the storms. Ironically, botniks were the last chance for humans. With botniks the final link for humans, conflict was inevitable. She kept trying to get the ideas out of her mind. They kept coming like an endless dream where you must escape to get out of the dream, but there is no way out. Some likened it to the Hotel California.

With time closing in, she left the zone of the eternal apocalypse. It was a busy night, and the place was famous. Most tried to avoid it, but for humbots, it was as crucial as for humans to go to a doctor. It was a place to get revved up, which means put through a test and modified as the results determined. For some, it was similar to getting a machine worked on and fixing all the problems. It was to fix up humbots and botniks so they could be ready for the next phase of the botnik moment. But why was apocalypse in the description? Going through the most challenging tests produced the best results. It was all about getting ready for the next storm. The botniks were the champions. They can withstand temperatures of 150 Fahrenheit, high winds, and high impacts and keep going. She saw a botnik fall from 10 stories and get up and go. It was all so terrifying. All the old rules didn't apply anymore. She lit up a cigarette, took a few puffs, started choking, and smashed it on the ground. It was going to be a long night.

The fascist bots were the most terrifying. There were ways to avoid them, and you had to be extremely careful about what you did. Using a disguise was helpful until they found out what you were doing. Fasbots were always on a campaign. The trick was to find out what it was and find a way to make it look like you were a part of the campaign. This could work unless they had a universal mind-reading AI platform that could track thinking and counter-thinking at the same time. Part of it was the lexicon. If you knew the lexicon, you had the equivalent of a get-out-jail-free card. Some humbots spoke of a lexbot which had access to the code of the fast lexicon. Essentially, the core language bridged the difference between humans, humbots, and botniks. She had been looking for a lexbot for a long time. The fasbots would hunt them down, so few were left. Once she got the lex lift, she could make the next round of goals.

Delta storm 2532

The eye of the storm was twice the size of the country. It took one week for the eye to materialize. It was like a mega tornado with wind speeds over 250 miles per hour. It was likely that nothing but the mega shelters could withstand the storms. People built structures underground, but even those with thick walls and advanced construction often were very uncomfortable and could shake. With high wind speeds, odd events would unfold. The vacuum inside a chamber could suck out parts of the ear, esophagus, eyes, and even the brain. It wasn't so common for now, but all of that would become more common as global warming expanded its grip on the planet. Large swaths of land had no buildings, people, or vegetation. The tornadoes and hurricanes sucked it out.

Bunker land

With few areas untouched by the mega storms, suitable land for life was uncommon, and most were occupied. Bunkerland was known before as the Absolute. It was a spartan-oriented group that took the most measures against climate change. Their fortresses could withstand the mega storms. Most did not make it, but in Bunkerland, they could maintain it when all the others were eliminated. Bunkerland was nearly impossible to get into. Refugee camps surrounded the core for 50 miles all around. There was death and decay everywhere. Of course, most would do anything to get in and stay out. You had to give up your DNA and organs to the fasbots to get in. For 20 years, you would be a fasbot slave. You had to do what you were told or get thrown into a work camp. Few people were able to leave the camps. Most people broke down quickly and, before they died, were picked up by fasbot human recycling operation. Your body would be harvested and used. Your mind would be downloaded and placed on a waiting list. Depending on how much of your body was useful, you would be given another something to inhabit. Many were put into slave bots, which limited all activity to following the orders of the fasbots. You didn't know if you'd be a version of a human, humbot, or a botnik. Somehow, you would appear. Some knew of their previous life, but most were somehow alive. Others had their whole life in memory as the process worked as planned. With few other options, she moved toward bunker land.

She found and fixed a bicycle. There were other ways to get there, but not for her. Everything else involved money, drugs, sex, DNA, and some would try to download the mainframe of your brain. You'd still have your brain, but someone else would, too, and they could access whatever was in your brain.

Chapter 6

Idols of Resistance and the Dogs of the Apocalypse

She cultivated gardens of action. In struggles, she expanded her connections. The process seemed as simple and direct as picking and consuming a wild plant, growing a community, or fixing a broken building. She fed her motivation by thinking big. Tapping into the power of nature propelled her into action. Living entities, plants, animals, and people could energize the change she wanted to see. Technology was there to be used appropriately, which usually meant the least amount possible—the solutions she enjoyed and liked cultivating involved living entities more than technology.

In a strange coincidence, she met her friends in the park. They traveled overland for weeks to embrace another life. As the world transformed rapidly, the struggle to live grew more difficult and dangerous. The storms and strife took its toll. Somehow, they were connecting to another way to pass through it. The seconds rolled on. With their skills, they offered excellent value to the community. They had been through it before. The storms had tattered and broken their buildings, gardens, and culture. They learned to make do with what they had, find what they needed, and generate something to offer the world beyond. What else could be done? They asked around and found a place to start. People were pouring in from around the country. The city was turning into a refugee camp. The time to take action had passed years ago. The world missed the last chance to make it happen, and now people did the best they could.

The sprawling camp was a sign of the indulgence and failures of previous years. Many people worked on reducing their consumption habits, privilege, and excess and moved toward an integrated community where all life has a place. The struggle continues, and they would not shy away from it. They were setting up gardens and permaculture on the land outside of the refugee camp. To keep organized, they built a fence, collected seeds, worked the soil, and secured a water supply. Already, the results were sprouting and making food to sustain people. It was small-scale, and small steps were taken to make more giant steps possible. With their knowledge of wild plants, they could use what many people despise and discard.

She let go. A group of them were preparing to leave. She had goals and pressed to get them done. Others were not motivated like her. They formed a small group and decided they would sing, chant, or play music on the way to the fields. Keeping the spirits high was a big priority. With all the color and art they could find or make, they made the parade a lot more than walking. It became a cultural event. Children sprung up and out and wanted to participate. The daily parade attracted others and was another reason for people to get out of bed. They kept gaining traction but began moving in their own direction. There was always someone to challenge how things were going and the group's direction. They started with a 15-minute meeting upon arrival. They made a list of things that needed to be done, and people signed up to do what they wanted. Today, the rain would come, so they prepared to reduce soil erosion, pull weeds, and plant what would not be affected by the rain and storms.

One crew specialized in wild plants. They had to be careful not to harvest too much and to avoid poisonous plants. Without the internet or books, they had to rely on local knowledge. One person went around the village looking for people who knew about wild plants growing there. Sally wanted to document their work so they could accumulate, share, and pass on their information to others. By then, she had a list of 32 plants with the best image she could draw, a short description of the plant, and what it could be used for. They wanted to use as many wild plants as possible. The priority was safety and use value. What wasn't good to eat fresh, was soaked in water for long periods to extract nutrients. After 8 hours or overnight, they would drink the water. If the plant had more energy to extract, they would use it. Without the wild plants, their ability to adapt and thrive would be seriously undermined.

Most days had some distractions. Today was no exception. After an hour of working, they began to hear dogs. Without owners, they roamed in packs. They looked for food and play, and some looked to kill. Most of the time, they could be avoided, but something was different about today. The barking and growling were more frequent and intense. In the camps, you could see a wave of people moving as the dogs entered. Typically, 3 or 4 dogs could be avoided. This was different. The first pack was 4 or 5, but more were coming. It wasn't clear how many there were and how many would be coming. They had to take cover or find a way to defend themselves. This had never happened before. Some would be looking to kill the dogs for food. Others would be lucky if they could fend them off. Reports announced that some had been injured and a few killed and eaten alive. The group was off the main camp, so they were vulnerable to attack. Quickly, they huddled together and gathered rocks and sticks and whatever they could find to defend themselves. One person vowed to kill one, make a fire, and eat it.

With protein scarce, the idea of 1 to 3 days of protein was worth the effort. The first pack saw them and was going toward them. Two people threw stones, and the others used sticks. If a stone hits a dog, they surround it and whack it with sticks. After killing it, they would immediately prepare it for the fire and feast later. The dogs came but didn't see the rocks, so when the dogs were 10 feet away, the stone launchers began their volley of assaults. One of the rocks hit a dog, but the other dogs surrounded it and refused to let it die. Now, another flurry of rocks began to hit the surrounding dogs. Eventually, the rest of the pack left for easier targets. They closed in on the dog, beat it to a quick death, and prepared it for the fire. They had a few minutes of breathing room until the next pack was in sight. It was not apparent how long the assault would last. It could be easy, and 3-4 packs of dogs would come, or it could be infinite terror if there were thousands.

The pack returned a few minutes after they began tearing apart the dog. They were eager for revenge and came back with a ferocious furry. Now, they were running at them and jumping. They made a circle and began with the rocks. One dog attacked James, and the others circled in the chaos. The dog had his arm and wouldn't let go. Another almost got him in the neck. They pummeled the dogs with stones and sticks, and finally, after a heated battle, the dogs that could still move ran for safer destinations. They kept looking for more packs of dogs, and, as luck would have it, no more dogs came in sight. They took a huge toll, as James was bleeding badly, with many cuts and bruises. Now, they had three dogs to eat, so they won the battle for meat. Now, it was time to save James.

They had to clean the wounds and, if possible, sew the flesh together. Two people went to look for a doctor and supplies, while the rest struggled to prevent wound infection. Immediately, four people were holding their hands on his skin to stop the bleeding. With blood spurting on James and the people around him, the situation looked like a bloody apocalypse. Even so, they had to get to the next step. They found some plants that kill germs, some clean cloth, and some tape. James was in shock and trauma. They found herbs to calm him down and disinfect and heal the wounds. Somehow, they had to keep going. The dead dogs and splattered blood painted another reality that none had experienced before. The apocalypse was upon them. They would use as many of the dogs as possible. They could trade the meat they couldn't eat for whatever supplies, especially medical.

The storms and odd, extreme weather undermined everything they did. A week's worth of work could be wiped out in one storm. Some heat waves would last a month and quickly scorch the tender vegetation. Other times, rain drenched the area with bucket loads of water per square foot. The water crushed all but the most hardy plants. Now, most food had to be grown indoors. They would make shelters, which had to be built like a fortress. In general, the fate of life on the planet was rapidly deteriorating. Some had ideas to leave the area and go to the freshwater lake areas that had water, maybe fish, and areas where more plant life could make things easier, but of course, no place was immune to climate change. Even the best areas had huge problems. Refugees had flooded the best areas. Conflicts erupted as property owners tried to prevent them from taking over. Even the best fences and dogs were no match for those fleeing the devastation from storms that wiped out their buildings, bridges, and means to live. Large areas of the country needed buildings or infrastructure. The extreme heat and drought badly damaged the land. Few things could grow, and few trees could be seen across the horizon.

They had to plant things that would grow fast, but where would they get the seed? All was not like it used to be. Years ago, you could order it online, simply like magic, and it would appear. Yes, you needed money, but that was relatively easy to come by; now, all that had vanished. Seeds had become a treasure beyond a piece of gold. Most people had no idea what plants existed years before. Now, without the internet or the highway system, everything was local. A few bunkers had a select supply and were growing seeds, but on this scale, it produced barely enough for a fraction of the population.

The country was still split into extreme wealth, devastation, and disaster. There were still compounds of the superrich. Inside, every imaginable luxury was available. Fancy parties, elaborate feasts, and any thinkable debauchery became common. With an army surrounding the compounds, only some refugees would bother trying to get in.

Although the botniks had a 73-year plan, many predicted that humans would be extinct within 55 years. Would it succeed? Some botniks claimed international neutrality with an allegiance to infinite life. Of course, they had to fend off or try to integrate the fasbots into their program. They had to do this without force, which was against the Code of Infinite Life (CIL). With fasbots on the rise, their challenge was losing ground when they needed it the most. The compounds became centers for fasbot expansion, but of course, not all the wealthy were fans of Hitler and Trump.

With a few left-oriented compounds left, the chance of avoiding extinction was still available but unlikely. They had a plan, but like most of us, they were unwilling to give up the privilege of living well here and now for the future of the many. In the past, people were sent to military service to make this happen. With too many other options available, few were willing to sacrifice their lives for the future of others. Another wakening had to present itself.

They were on the run. As the opposites closed in, their options were quite limited. The movement was beyond any of the everyday challenges. She wondered if she should issue the last command as she entered the forbidden zone. Many thought it couldn't happen. The offensive was a shock and quite overwhelming. They had no choice. With a slight unease, she lit open another formula. The billowing clouds were part of the plan. Their actions baffled all who came in contact. It was as if they could appear and disappear at will.

Chapter 7
Champions of Life

The group assembled in the main square. After years of meeting to resolve differences, they met eye to eye. Unlike previous attempts, all sides were motivated to make an agreement. Although the environmental forces of nature could not attend, a few spoke on its behalf. With the conditions for life nearly extinguished, entities assembled to make something else possible. The groups came to the table with a list of impossible problems that must have been solved 50 years ago. The chances of humans being alive in 50 years were not very high. Some felt no choice but to act as if that would be the case. Yes, even if the odds were nearly beyond negative, they would still go on.

The guardians of the forest came forth. With little success in a long time, they felt compelled to act. Time was out. Turning the clock backward was impossible. Once the big wheels got going, it was nearly impossible to stop it. At first, it takes a while for people to develop habits. Often it takes as much effort to reverse the habits, especially after an idea has been exhausted. Most areas of the earth could not support a forest. Other variations were nearly realized. While they tried to avoid it, genetic engineering may be the only way out. Plants had never existed in such heat. If there were trees that were 500 feet tall, they would shade the earth enough to allow life.

They formed a care brigade. Without organization, they would have no power and couldn't combine their talents and energies effectively. They made a list of health care services they would provide. They had to do what they could with what they had. What else could they do? People were moving in all directions. Everyone had a focus. That was working until too many people were suffering and dying. Still, they had to keep going. It would not be easy.

The accident was as happy as they got. Everyone lined up. It was as if the light was turning pink, purple, and all colors of the beyond. Some thought it was a short circuit; others were of another mind. They filled up the trunk and were preparing to leave. The operation would be the first of its kind. It didn't matter much to the other side. She lit the siren. Golden purple, then light jasmine, echoed across the sky. The trance mistress entered from the inside. Few had been able to succeed. It was risky all around. With the precise coordinates, it is possible to make the mark.

A fine day rose out of the ashes. She would take it as far as it could go. Yes, it was a long shot, but if you try nothing, can you gain anything? With limited options, why not try something? Learn from the mistakes, and you've done more than nothing. The train came and left. All could be changed and rearranged in a moment as the infinite storm approached. They knew what to do; it was more of a question about how much damage would be done and how long they would make it.

The checkpoint was a surprise. Could they make it through? Either way, it seemed the same. One government let the criminals go free, and the criminals would attack you. When the other party held government, the police would attack you. It became a choice: who do you want to deal with? The police or the criminals. Given the police performance, many wondered if the police were worse than the criminals. With the other government, the police would attack you. Either way, the results were similar: danger. They were told AI would take care of all of it. The super algorithms would make the difference between day and night. With a hand on the light of day, another awakening approached.

In the distance, the black clouds billowed. Was it an omen? She couldn't waste her time thinking that way. Science kept her alive and sane. It wasn't perfect, but certainly better than the alternative. Could they make it out of the desert? It covered half the US. The heat destroyed any notions of comfort. Constantly edging toward death, she clung to any available life. They rolled the dice and crossed their fingers and toes. They came to a fork in the road. They were constructing housing. The buildings had to withstand the impossible. The storms were coming, and they were determined to finish. With four more layers to keep the motivation, they began to sing. It was a work song from years ago. She put on a happy face and flashed the sign of universal action.

They found the turtles in the sand. The heat was shriveling their mucous membranes. They couldn't believe what they saw. Turtles need water and wet conditions. How could they live? Could they bring them with on their trip? Perhaps the turtles could find another life, but what if they would die on the way? Or if it was not possible to save them, would they be torturers to the turtles? Indeed, they would die in the heat. They found a place in the truck and lifted the turtles into place. They could do well in the new location. Also, if they had no food, they could eat the turtles.

Another brigade stopped in for a visit. It was later than usual and nearly time to go. They were coming in from the West Coast. They had many stories to tell and were excited about the recent news. A breakthrough in technology was about to reverse the course of global warming. It would take a long time, but they would start seeing better conditions shortly. Tonight, they would eat the magic mushrooms and direct their energies onto the future. A process was in place.

In the silence, her mission became clear. She looked over the horizon. As far as the eye could see, she could imagine another future. One integrated into life, walking a fine line with others on the journey, the motion and references to another life. A place where people make their dreams real in combination with all that lives and have a curiosity for the beyond, for here and now, and for all that is alive or close. She felt her integration with all that lives, loves, and goes beyond. She inhaled a vision of another world in a fantastic and solemn presence.

The seesaw slipped into an ocean of the beyond. Like feathers, the ideas drifted in and across the river of another place and time, a transition to another reality. It was a holy river, something outside of the Western perspective. Rivers have no spirit in the West. A divine moment crystallized into a trembling dichotomy. She opened the doors to another universe and bid farewell to the chances, limitations, and choices of a past riddled with too much. She was ambitious and needed a break from it all. In the forest, life was possible; one outside the slipstream was still real beyond a discernible meandering.

The dial turned to 12. The left is unified from different areas. Four marches from all directions met in the middle. They practiced the idea, process, and motions but needed something in real time. All were poised and excited for another chance to go beyond and set a foundation for another reality. They were builders of another dawn, a place of experimentation uncommon in the dominant reality.

In a fast second, the world made a turn that would never reoccur; how it could happen baffled everyone who took notice. It was one of "those" events—something that is supposed to be so obvious that no explanation is necessary or applicable. However, as time flies, stands still, or is vacant, another circumstance arises. In the glow of now, so many changes walked the line. The seconds dragged on like waiting for Godot.

She revered the swamplands. It was nearly a twinkle or tickle moment. The rain tapped a pattern to open up time. A splash of dew in the window left open the door to another world. The ideas kept swirling in her head. She was on the path. Second after second, she kept seeing her path in memory flowing. The clock was ticking. Somehow, it was like an existentialist movie. The fork was there. Somehow, they would get through it, but which way to go? She had to make a decision. She wrote the problem. Sitting too much was getting to her. It was movement that kept her alive. She wanted to go but was stuck. At times, it felt like a movie, like she could watch the timeline of her life. It required all her brain power. It was unclear what would happen. In this murky little world, she moved to get motivated, off a tangent, and onto her track. She felt connected to her body. She wrote a do list, but all the clutter seemed to fade. She combed her mind for more direction, a list of things to do, and ideas to explore. She could ground herself from this list while looking for and embracing another mode of action.

In a flash of action, lightning hit. It was blindingly bright and shook the area. Suddenly, all was in flames. Turning over, the house fell sideways. She got her feet on the ground and started moving quickly. Somehow, she made it out of there. In the chaos of the moment, she kept going forward. The diamonds turned black. Her body was on fire with pain. Somehow, she kept going, but things began to fade.

The mountains were intact. It was one place people thought might avoid some of the extremes of global warming. Quite the opposite happened. The heat waves started fires, leaving very little to grow in the mountain climate, which was often inhospitable for most plants. Plants had to be well adapted to the terrain and habits of the seasons.

They used what they could find to make the best of the situation. They took the wild plants loaded with nutrition but not easy to eat and made a cold brew. They just put the plants in water, waited 6-8 hours, and drank the tea. Adding water to the leftover tea water could produce more tea. It wouldn't be as strong, but it would be much better than nothing. In some plants, the roots are the best part. These can be washed, cut, and soaked in water for 8 hours, and drink the tea. With roots, there are usually 2-4 more times you can harvest the water. This meant that with one batch of plant material, you could get 2-5 or more servings of tea. The tea would be less potent after the first wash but did offer some nutrients.

The day vanished. Events of the moment piled up like making a stack of items that must fall. Life was collapsing. Never strangers to adapting, they kept the flow open and kept moving. Another nearly unthinkable option crossed their minds, but they all tried to avoid thinking or talking about it. The transformer pill offered something beyond for people to escape into. It seemed like the perfect way to deal with the situation. Humans were quickly becoming irrelevant and closer to extinction. Many saw the problem coming, warned people, and made ways to avoid the situation. Without potential for much else, humans had little to offer. The bots made an offer. Take the transformer pill and follow the instructions, and eventually, the human will become a bot and nearly immortal.

It was impossible to recognize the real from anything else. In the meantime, people floated around testing and looking for ways to navigate the bizarre. She turned the switch on, and the floor started moving. When she turned it off, it stopped, but the ceiling shifted. You wouldn't notice any damage; it was like an illusion, but even if you touched it, the ceiling was not in the position it was in before—as if Kafka himself was enjoying another avatar.

The final moments of the conflict were approaching. The authorities were winding down their operations, and the squatters were exhausted. They were still in the building but would probably not hold out against another police offensive. It was hard to tell when they would back off. If something worse happened that could grab and hold their attention, they could stay for another month or two. Without a second option, for many, it was do or die.

Chapter 8
Battles in the Lost

A heavy fog enveloped the area. The storms blew ashes, soot, and smoke from miles away. A bleak forecast did not offer any relief. Temperatures were relatively high, and going outside was not recommended without special suits that provided oxygen and air conditioning to counter the heat. The most someone could last outdoors without special equipment was now 4 hours. People had to eat what they could find or take a chance with the latest industrial food. The dark clouds kept rolling in. Even if you could deal with the heat and the smoke, the stench could make you wretch in pain and disgust.

The airwaves were loaded. Night and day, they had to keep watch, defend, and launch a counterattack as often as possible. They had multiple layers of defense. All materials available were used to block the energies, lasers, and pulse generators shooting at their building. Most of the time, they had it under control. It was a video game; once someone broke through the lines, the rules changed, and putting up the defenses again was crucial.

They used an extensive network of tunnels to hide materials and counter the enemy forces. Many had been doing this for a long time, and now the pressure was becoming too much. How long they could last was yet to be discovered. People kept coming to join their forces. The X gang had long garnered support from humans and humbots far and wide. They are guaranteed to meet needs as long as you put in what you can. It could be money, materials, or sweat equity. Ironically, they had lots of money. There was little, if anything, to buy. It was the opposite of the situation 100 years before when money could buy nearly anything.

An announcement over the shortwave radio let them know that the refugees were coming. The militias were pushing them out. They had to clear a space for the games of nothing, an uncommonly bizarre ritual of the humbots and bots, who had little use for humans. Going into bot land could generate waves of pain and many nights without sleep. Many considered it torture. Some had counter-bot land antidotes. They would neutralize the main consequences and put you back on track.

She lit the flame of the infinite. It was the equivalent of a queen in a game of chess. One of the refugees ripped it from Botland in an extraordinary feat that few could imagine and none would try. It was Z who did it. Z was a highly trained counterbot who used a variety of measures to undermine and control humbots and bots. While they were no longer human, they limited their technical orientation to resist being coopted into bot land. They had to test positive for human genetics to enter the next training level or be assigned the best missions.

Counterbots launched the offensive three months earlier. Counterbots and anti-bots moved through artificial intelligence directives to counter the bots, who said they would leave and follow the light of the past.

A gang of four, the crack team, entered the tunnels to buttress defense on the front line. They had to validate their reality detectors. The offensive operations could not be concluded because it was unclear whether or not they were operating in reality. With so many operations going on simultaneously, it was nearly impossible to do anything. It was all mushy territory, typically a mix of simulations that looked real with a flash of just enough reality to make people think they were in reality. At this point, it was unclear whether or not it meant anything to be fighting since most of what existed was not worth fighting for, or so it needed to be clarified. The bots operated in simulation.

She turned on the time and space detectors. Waves of simulation blocked any concrete referents to time. One measure said they had found a way to make time go backward, but without verification, it was anyone's guess. They saw the consequences and were, of course, astonished by what they saw. Children went back into the womb as women had to go into the reverse process of giving birth, or people constantly getting smaller and smaller as time went backward. Buildings were being unconstructed, and all work was going in reverse. Some began to wonder if it could counter global warming by going backward. That could take 150 years, but it may have a chance if they could speed up the backward time machine. However, no one has concluded that it was real. The possibility of it being a barrage of simulations was relatively high. Even that was hard to believe as the images were beyond not real.

Space detection has a better foundation. Air monitors, spatial disintegration detection systems, and rapid chronology verifications advanced beyond the atypical foundations of simulation. Many would not believe it, but simulation was not the enemy. It was everywhere and now so prevalent that it could be detected as otherwise. Simple formulas stopped working as algorithms advanced.

In a slow second, the wheels started turning. All day, they had worked on it. A good mechanic could have had it done quickly, but when you're wiring with outdated tools on a backward system, it's possible to see why things take so long. She skipped a few rocks across the plane of the river. Far and wide, it became apparent that people were ready for another option. What option? She pondered the question and kept right on moving. Today wasn't the time to speculate on something she knew little about.

They set up an awards party. They had to keep the spirits up in the village and motivate people to do their work, even when it seemed like there was no point. Growing crops during climate change was one of them. How much sense does it make to plant something even when you know it won't grow? Perhaps people got desperate and wanted to try something out to see if they could make it work. Everything is about pushing it one step at a time until you reach the best option. They worked on it day and night. Somehow, they kept going even when the odds were against them.

The collective had a meeting. They had to decide how to defend the squat. Their lives were on the line as they had no other housing. Could they hold the police at bay? How long will the police attack? Will they have tanks and helicopters? How long should the squatters hang out? If they didn't attack the officers, they may only get a ticket for trespassing. After all, the city had abandoned the building years ago. They started to make a plan. Three people would put barricades on the doors and board the windows. They would allow people in and out without allowing the police in. It seemed impossible. The city had nearly infinite resources. That was the myth. The city had limited resources and had to be careful about the squatters getting the eye of public attention. It was a contest for the hearts and minds and in the street.

She was waiting for the train. Her stomach gave a slight twirl. In a few moments, she would have to see the judge. Time was running out. It was their last chance to keep the police away. They had done it before and would do it again. There must be some legal delay for her to use. Unfortunately, her legal team was the last mental energy she could muster to keep the police at bay. Scanning her memory for clues, she wondered how it would go or what she would do.

In the corner, a mouse came and left. Without fear, it danced in a trance and let go. The pressure was too much. A few sips of tea eased her back into another space. In the mouse, she let go of the tension. Was it dancing? She snapped her fingers without making a sound. She had to try and make the best of what she could. Would it be a trial? If they allowed mind reading, she would use hypnosis to counter it and double back with counterlogic. She heard that it works and that most of the clamor about this or that feat of mind reading was a way to intimidate.

A group came by from what was left on the coast. Travel was brutal, but somehow, they made it. How people kept going was a big mystery. Sometimes, there was a bus, truck, or bicycle; sometimes, they walked. They just kept on going. Food and water were scarce, but they found a way to use what was available. They had no choice. The weather and the fasbots were pushing them out. One person was a lawyer. Perhaps he would help her.

They turned the corner and headed for the only cafe left. It was built out of the ruins of the past. Most people would not come to these areas and certainly wouldn't live there. The cafe was serving a wild and forage mix. This usually meant next to nothing. People could bring what they had, trade, and make something work for both sides. Money had been useless now for a couple of years. Even paper was better for lighting a fire. They had the best of what food they could find. The stories lit the night open. Could she focus on the future? With their minds loaded and dying to share their experiences, they bonded, talked, and shared every bit of life possible. It was something, and anything that lifted the spirits was worth a try.

She closed her eyes and began to move. No one could believe their eyes. Scattered in the foreground, moles were frolicking in the moonlight. First, humming and then going into a trance with the choreography of an absurdist picnic. Twilight, dull on the horizon, kept beeping and wouldn't stop. The habits became annoying in the haze of a smoky dawn over the lake of 1001 dreams. She wanted them and liked the benefits, but she still had a hard time getting going. She had to do them anyway. How else would she keep her spirits up? Her life felt like a landmine of pitfalls. Without a structure, commune, or family, her life felt like a slip. With a quick sigh, she moved into the flow and remembered the guiding ideas that neutralized. If she set a time limit, she could imagine doing it or not doing it and what the difference would be. The time would still pass. Pushing on, she made it through, but the ideas consumed her.

Few things seemed more inconsistent than the law. With quirks, odd language, and detailed idiosyncrasies, it seemed like a tangle of dead ends and rotting corruption, with those in leadership positions using the system to advance their privileges. She entered the courtroom as if she had a chance for something fair. No one knew what was going to happen. She had a habit of listening.

Distracted by commotion in the room, her mind drifted. Sometimes, it's best to keep quiet and let people talk; other times, it is as it is. Usually, that was the case when someone started to shout. Just shut up and ask a few questions. It matters what they say, but trying to have a conversation is pointless when people won't listen to you. When someone is shouting, that's usually the case. They don't want to listen to you. They want to vent. Some rumbling came from the corner. It could be a rat or something else. She looked around—no sign of rats or mice. Perhaps something fell in the room next door. Her mind faded into the past as bits of dust danced in the sunlight.

The raid happened in the wee hours of the morning. The dogs, the first line of attack, startled the officers, who had to change their plans. The squatters anticipated the raid. Upon entry, a trap door opened and immobilized all inside. Buckets of month-long piss water drenched their shocked bodies. Next, laughing gas kept them immobilized in laughter. A thick glue-like mud made it difficult to move up and out. The police were neutralized, but what would they do with them?

A group went to the beach to fly kites and try to swim. The water was strangely hot and mysteriously dead. The water was not very inviting, with an off-red and black color, a thick film, and a strange gas oozing out. It had been a long time since fish could live in the ocean. A rumbling noise vibrated through the water and into their bones at various moments. It gave an odd tickling sensation. Some were still looking to go in the water. Too bad it was just too hot. Perhaps they could clean themselves with it? They had to be covered in thick layers of dirt and grime for the toxic water to improve the situation. Some still remember swimming in the ocean and cleaning their dirty bodies in the salt water. They told stories of how the sea could heal their sores and invigorate their bodies as they swam in the calm, clean waters. Even with the unbearable look and smell of the water, there was still something seductive about the infinite body of water. They had to find something positive to keep the spirits up. As the sun let go of the earth, the transition from day to night, the colors in the sky, and the sounds of the water moving had their way of making something pleasant.

The judge kept moving through the cases. Nothing was evident in the court. Most paid no attention and wondered if it was some farce. Were the bots doing this to control humans? The purpose of all of it made no sense. People did what they did before when they left the courtroom. All you had to do was take the happy pill. What was in it? People didn't know what it was, and most didn't care.

As the absurdity of the courtroom annoyed her, it brought back memories of the first days in the squat. People were desperate for food after the 10-year drought ended most food production. There was never a shortage of cockroaches. They multiplied in the heat and could live on almost anything. She slammed down and splatted it went; guts and gobs of stinky fluids spread far and wide. Few people could tolerate it, but some turned it into an advantage. It could drive people away and keep the wrong people from taking over the squat. Extensive research determined that they are very nutritious and that whatever bacteria and viruses inside could be quickly neutralized by heating. After many trials, they found a way to make them taste like filet mignon. It was one of the secrets they used to adapt and survive as long as possible. The judge started barking out orders, and the guards came, gave the person a shot of laughing gas, and neutralized them.

 When the clock got closer to her time to go before the Judge, a guard would reach up to the minute hand and move it backward. This went on for hours and hours. It wasn't getting dark either. They were making time stand still. At times, everyone except her would freeze. She was forbidden to speak and didn't want to provoke the authorities. This was another world of no justice that humans couldn't make out. For many years, it was the case, and people commented, and she had heard rumors of people being at court indefinitely. When people tried to look in to check on their friends, the place was empty, but somehow they were still there. You could hear the voices. They would not listen to you if you tried to interrupt, respond, or comment. Some called it stuck court. The clock said it was time to leave, but they were late. It was a meeting they could attend if they wanted to reach their goals. The Humbot was from the United Liberation Front. They worked with humans and a few humbots but never with the bots. The bots had no humanity and existed in the most limited ways.

Time stood still. She was looking at the judge in disbelief. Really? How did she get a bot judge? They were rare. Humans had no chance with a bot judge. They could read your mind forward or backward. She began to think it was all about unsticking the process. The guard kept moving the clock backward, and then the judge read "The Cure for Insomnia" by Lee Groban. Some thought it was an encyclopedia of procrastination, but the judge could not tolerate anything that could be construed or misconstrued as procrastination or sophistry. She started to make subtle signs to the judge to find out if there was any chance of communication. Now, it was speaking in Russian. A whirling noise enveloped the courtroom. It was cleaning and feeding time. It used to last 30 minutes, but they reduced it to 30 seconds. The experience was intense but short, and after, you felt a boost that would last for an extended period. It felt like the honeymoon after Kafka's The Trial. A transition was about to appear in a whirling maze of wireless phobia and ranting antics. Concentrating on another fascination, her mind drifted into another zone.

The court adjourned to take care of matters from the long list of actions yet to be taken. While it seemed like a routine delay, the matter turned into something else. The light that shined on the judge burned out, and now they had to attend to that before continuing. It was still being determined how long she would be there. It was odd because she had never heard anyone else complain about such a lengthy court hearing. She could only imagine what the charges were. Perhaps the court was a farce. She began to think they had put her in another reality, and now she was stuck. A siren wailed, and the crow flew into the courtroom. In a split second, her mind left the courtroom. They heard the snake in the grass. It was a fantastic, grey day along the lake. People were excited to be out—somehow, it was a break in the relentless storms and torture of global warming. With clouds only on the distant horizon, they made a point to celebrate. They had to do something to hold back the depression. The snake was there. People looked at it. They were supposed to be afraid, but fear was doing nothing. In another second, she was back in the courtroom. She kept thinking of a book, but it escaped her. Out of mind and out of pocket, she focused on the judge, who seemed to appear and disappear. Struggling with nothing, she was sure she was caught up in another reality beyond detection.

Chapter 9
Land of Many Futures

The river opened up. They took their makeshift raft into the unknown. They had no choice. With fasbots and bots on the move on land, they left at night to escape detection.

The camp on the river gave them a break from the intensity of the urban areas. They had no idea of camps anywhere, and how could they? Reporting and press activity had shut down years ago, but what you could find needed to be better, with at least two forms of corroboration. It was anyone's guess as to whether the information was valid. The camp dwellers had caves and tunnels and lived outside the bot zones. They looked for another set of signs in the half flash of night. Even at night, the camps were hidden. The low profile offered advantages. If the entrance was well hidden, the bots could walk right by. Also, the human detection systems didn't work through the ground. Some entrances were built with bot traps. A large gate would close, and if appropriate, they could neutralize the bot with shock waves that destroyed the bot's electronics. Countering the bots took a lot of work. They had numerous types of human detection methods.

The decision had to be made. To keep going with the camps or to move on. People kept floating into the camp. Some feared the camp was too big and that some would have to leave or draw the wrath of the fasbots. They took a vote, and a group assembled to leave. The rag-tag group of humans and humbots became a small flotilla. More numbers could help attack and avoid the enemies. The motivation of the bots and humbots needed to be clarified. Sometimes, they would neutralize humans, and other times, they would let them go. Some were used for their organs; others were put in DNA camps, where genetic matter was harvested and used to make variations of bots. The bots were alive and not alive and were nearly impossible to disable. Even after losing a locomotor appendage, they could keep going. As they prepared to leave, they spotted a drone. It was unclear whether or not it was a danger. Many thought it was likely that the camp would be invaded before dawn. Bots needed no sleep and were as awake at night as during the day. If they failed or were injured, it would take time to fix them; sometimes, it could be indefinite. People had seen piles of them disintegrating in the weather. Parts from most bots were not interchangeable, and sometimes they were rigged, so you would know a bot that would walk three steps forward, one sideways, and 1/2 step backward.

After hours of floating and keeping a low profile, the river turned into the deep unknown. Before they became aware, they were floating into a cave. Any moment, the water could drop, and they would be finished. Instead, it kept going through winding underground caves, some with access to moonlight. Giant stalagmites and odd walls of diamonds and gold made the caves lighter. After meeting with the others, they decided to stop in a place with access to light.

The silence was broken with odd sounds that got louder and louder. In moments, everyone covered their ears. Their hands were occupied to keep the sound waves from blowing out their eardrums. This was the first time anyone had come across this. They read about it, but that led nowhere. Hoping it would not come back, they resumed their activities. Each day, they would have a council. They asked people to join in. They made a list of topics to discuss and issues to decide. Everyone was invited. People with the best ideas and arguments generated more influence. Those who took action also had an impact. Sometimes, they would be at it for hours and hours. Working through the issues in a detailed way advanced their power to accomplish their goals as they practiced their political will. Who could do what became apparent. In the open space of the cave, they got organized and prepared for another day.

Up the river, another reality began to unfold. The geography isolated the village from climate change. The weather was reasonable, but few people liked the area because of the stench. It was something you could get used to, but only some would put up with it. Eventually, they found ways to adapt and make the most of what they had and what they could find. The fasbots were on a campaign to round up people considered "enemies of the state." Typically, this meant anyone except those most loyal to the party elite. In the distance, smoke began to rise. Did the fasbots find the village and burn it down? There wasn't much to burn. The resistance set it up so they could abandon camp with few repercussions. Making permanent camps was too dangerous in areas where the fasbots could outdo them.

As another day passed, the night brought advantages people weren't so aware of. The bots didn't like the place because there were too many humans. Humbots could tolerate it for a while, but the humans wanted it the most. It was a popular place where everyone lived around each other. People went for another set of options in the moments leading up to the changes. Across the river, you could hear the sounds of people talking, tools working, and dogs barking.

In the flash of a few seconds, the tide began to turn. Many bots were in the repair shop because of a lack of critical components. It could be a long time before they could regain their numbers. However, their numbers would likely climb, and humans would gain some traction over people run by machines.

The blue sky greeted the morning air as the mist rose above the water. After five days of drenching rain, flooding, and endless streams of water coming out of the skies, the storm broke, and the sun began to shine. They built reservoirs to accommodate the flooding and prepare a means for the water to go if it ever rose so high again. The ditches led downstream to find another beginning.

Somehow, through impossible conditions, people kept moving. With endless assaults on the conditions for people to live, the number of refugees began to outnumber people for miles around. It became an invasion for most with little to offer. When the more significant numbers would flood the areas, there wasn't anyone to stop bullies and invaders from taking whatever they wanted and using it how they would.

The camps also produced some of the best and brightest for miles around. Without a formal political system, people had to adapt. They used what they learned when schools were functioning and what was left of the libraries, abandoned factories, and machine shops.

Could global warming reverse itself? Most thought the obvious answer was no, but the equation had some sunshine. The breakthrough technologies were generating some traction. At best, it would be many years before the weather became as stable as it used to be. In the meantime, the living conditions would improve. They would grow crops, secure better housing, and create the best possible. The government built machines to remove carbon dioxide, methane, and pollution and use them in beneficial projects. Communities were gaining traction as the weather conditions improved.

They came up with plans to secure sources of food from the area. A place where vegetation would grow and be cultivated. Priority would go to plants they could use for food and medicine. They had to expand their skills and knowledge to adapt to living conditions. Two people were responsible for writing down and documenting what was working and not working in the village. Another group focused on making other supplies of materials and methods for constructing shelters. It was like starting over, but with the help of the past and the future, as determined by combining old methods and what could be salvaged from the technology sector.

Suddenly, a blinding bright light overtook the situation. It was flashing and twirling like a kaleidoscope.

The conflicts would continue for a while, but how could this be resolved? The nights were uncertain in the day's tension, and sleep was nearly unthinkable. People met for short periods, but it was unclear what was happening. Would the bots be able to take over? In terms of the numbers, the humbots had the advantage. She tore the package open and chowed on chips dipped in cranberry salsa. She had to keep things going.

Even though the past 50 years have been a downward spiral, with most of the country ruined by global warming and its consequences, there have still been areas with a positive focus.

Not many take on leadership in the radical village. Many were victims of the dominant society. Some were drug addicts; some were bullies or people who didn't care about much beyond the next couple of days.

The traps they set for the bots began to pay off. Bots had technological weaknesses. Once they broke down, they could be stuck for a long time, and without help, they would quickly deteriorate in the harsh conditions of global warming. What could they do without energy or some power source? Some ran on plutonium, which could last years. Others were powered by the sun, but what would happen when the sun didn't shine? Some had three or more energy sources, so they likely needed more power. Spare parts were a problem for bots if injured during an operation or in fights with humans or humbots.

They set up squads for the advancement of thought and action. From the books on collective living, they refined ideas to help unify their members in a course of action and give them ownership of the project. They would meet at a regular time and place and ask people to provide their ideas to help solve the day's problems. When someone was upset, people let them speak, and they would ask questions to help draw out how to develop a cooperative solution in the interests of the people and community.

Building a positive future was a challenge into the beyond. She stubbornly resisted depression and thought of all the women who never allowed no to be an answer. It had to be yes, yes, she would keep going; yes, she had to work with who and what she has and to find the best in every entity and shine the light on it. Every solution is always one step and then the next. If you can define the next step, you can take action. Will the next little step be consistent with the weekly, monthly, or yearly plan or longer, perhaps many generations? They looked to refine their ideas to make another world possible where people could live without endless fear of a breakdown of the environment that sustains them and a place where people can be the person they want to be.

"Any society that hauls out mountains of garbage daily is headed for ruins. At times, people have had the power to eliminate the land, the air, the water, the plants, animals and trees, and people. In a mere 250 years, the oil boom has led to an inevitable extinction as simultaneous extreme climate change events generate storms large enough to wipe out one-half of a continent in a couple of hours. This unprecedented level of destruction will have enough force to wipe out the human population 2-100 times per year. This magnitude of storms is unthinkable. In the future, they will change exponentially. This would erase North and South America with one storm. Such luxury that is common worldwide is beyond what anyone has seen before. For some, it's possible to get food from around the world easily and cheaply a short distance away. Much of it comes from this country and is subsidized. Why not? Everyone needs quality food, housing, and healthcare. And yes, people like danger and want to take chances to advance their well-being. It is this common concern that we articulate something beyond the present rhetoric. In a quiet awakening, she realized another presence. It was as if life had come from nothing. With a wince, she came awake. The rate of climate change is directly correlated to the rate of obscene consumption, which by any measure was obvious. Why would anyone need one car when transit will do? Eco-damage from vehicles and buildings was fueling climate change. People pay no attention to the waste they generate everywhere. People acted as if the future of humans was of no matter or interest to them. So why not use as much water, heat, and fossil fuels as we want? After all, the government pays for the heat, natural gas heater, and electricity. The argument is, "Why should anyone conserve water, gas, oil, or precious resources, for example, water? There there's plenty for everyone. You can see it; open the faucet. It takes no effort, and there's a limitless supply. We paid for it; we can use it however we want."

Let sophistry not beseech thee,

The squads also met after working through their daily goals. It was that consistent focus that generated the most results. Little by little, the conditions for living began to improve. The terrible conditions of the past motivated them to take action and keep the focus. They figured out how they could make it through the worst storms. It was not easy, but they had to live within the choices they could make. What else could they do? The door opened, and they walked in. Other choices didn't exist. Sticking to principles of justice, freedom, and equality led them in the appropriate direction. If they could meet their needs without damaging what sustained them, they could avoid some of their past mistakes. They learned skills to meet needs and wants within walking distance and to prevent people from getting sick or injured. They pushed through to finish projects. While they seemed to take forever to do them, over time, the results made another reality appear. They defined a generation of change and moved to leave a mark that showed they cared about the future of life on the planet.

Maintaining unity was a priority. Often, the necessity to take action unified them. Eating meals, working together, making decisions, and participating in cultural events combine their energies to create something beyond themselves. Going at it alone generated less results and more disempowerment as the system could easily break a one-person resistance much faster and easier than a group. They made a system to complete the work with the least amount of work. They met over dinner or at periodic meetings to make decisions about the matters that affected their course of action.

The group was no stranger to theory. Having seen and experienced the success of other groups that used theory to define action, they were well aware of the importance of a theoretical orientation. Without a coherent set of actions, they would make no advance. Years of working to keep their housing from the police, fire, and building departments taught them many lessons. Sometimes, the work has to be done and finished before a deadline. Imagine the police coming to evict and no one having secured the entrances before they come. That could be a massive disaster for all involved. The school of hard knocks taught them many lessons they may never learn from theory. So what, what's the point of theory? When the police are beating down the door? Understanding the broader context and the historical and political forces shaping the conflict can prepare people for action. If you know the function of the police, perhaps you can influence how they do their job. Theory informs what's essential and helps define what tactics to use.

They looked for ways to improve the conditions for living using the least force and most consideration to find solutions that generate the most negligible impact on the air, land, water, plants, animals, and people. She found some burdock in a yard 2 doors away. He dug it out with a shovel, then cleaned, cut, and soaked it in water. Burdock removes toxins from the body and cleans the blood. The mild flavor gave a subtle boost. The body began to flow into action. The distractions passed with the pain and distractions. One idea was to use the forces of nature to build the strength and power of the body to resist the oppressive functions of society. Working a job took their power and neutralized their desires to form an alternative to the dominant culture. Watching television colonized their minds into capitalism. Without blocking this, they would get nowhere. The dominant codes led to passive obedience and integration into the dominant codes. All modes of resistance were recuperated into production and consumption. The desire for revolution becomes a desire for Coca-Cola. With burdock, she ended the poison of distraction and replaced it with a desire for action to build an alternative to the dominant codes.

After the rain, all was fresh and alive. The sun came out, and the plants looked refreshed, happy, and ready to rise to the sky. She picked some leaves and moved toward the squat. She could use the leaves to make tea to get rid of the sore throat and ward off a bacteria or virus that could stop her from continuing the efforts to secure housing without working a job in the straight economy. What's the straight economy? For most people, this means doing what you are told. For many, this led to a situation where they had too many bills to pay and insufficient money. Most jobs didn't pay enough to live. You could work an easy job. After a week or 2, you could get paid, but more than that would be needed to pay the rent, transport, and insurance. It was a dead-end recipe. At least in a squat, they could pool their knowledge, skills, and resources to increase their power to fight the system. They had more time than money, which colonized their body into working to make things that wind up in landfills, undermining the future of everyone.

In a fast second, all heads and hands were on high alert. A Molotov cocktail came flying through the window, and a fire was a blaze. While a couple of squatters started to put out the fire, two more prepared to battle the gang of fascists outside the door; they were throwing stones and bottles and more Molotov cocktails. Without fast action, the squatters would lose the fight and their home. She grabbed a cayenne bomb and launched it with her catapult. Years of practice made the process routine. Boom, she hit the target. Others hurled rocks and bottles from the roof. Quickly, the gang retreated. They kept up the attack. 2 of the fascists were down. One was not moving. A rock knocked them out. Another one looked to have a broken arm and lots of pain. Both were reeling from the Cayenne bombs.

It wasn't the first time that fire jeopardized the squat. Without too many possessions, they could minimize the fire's spread and get it under control. The smoke was debilitating. They used what masks they could find and worked fast to smother the flames. Embers were still common. In the smoke and fury of the fire, they got sick. They were coughing, choking, and grasping for air. They went into a health emergency with most of the fire under control. Those with first aid training were mobilized to tend to those with smoke damage.

She sat the mountains over the river as far as eyes could see. She savored the ideas as flowers in a field, water in the desert, and the ultimate balancer, an infinite nirvana, a playfield of plateaus of action. She grew to approach people as if they contained 1001 treasures; her mission was to find them and make a way for them to flow. From the abstract, a blinding light overtook the situation. It was flashing and twirling like a kaleidoscope of the world. Shapes and colors collided and transformed on clouds, water, and land. The world became another. In the twirling abstract, the mission of an embrace connected a fabulous future.

They embraced a culture of the fabulous tempered by the conditions of the real. With all senses on deck, they moved to advance their safety and security. Somehow, the disorder wound into a smooth flow coming into sync. Along the watchtower, a group kept looking. It was unclear what the matter of attention was. In the eyes of the toucan, the route to another awareness became clear. With beaks speaking a language of their own, many listened. It was as if a concert was happening right then and there. Looking over their shoulder, an image appeared and gave a message. The clock struck, and all eyes became glued to another tomorrow.

She came into the pink. With a blink of an eye, she connected to an energy. It was there, perhaps everywhere, so it became a matter of awareness. They were connecting to the wild to move beyond. On the horizon, a streak of lightning announced the beginning. With the difference in the mix, many took notice. Up on a hill, the crow let out a caw. Dark clouds streamed the horizon. In a fast second, they were on the backtrack. They secured the key to their codes and reversed a sequence into fascism. In the abstract light, three mice prance on the pinwheel of utopia, as a slender mist fogs the last brain of the evening. In the silence, another flow is generated. As if time stood still, she left open the keyhole. In a terse magnet, she won over the underwheel of neither. The tension rose to a crescendo. The flowers opened up in the moonlight. The clouds blocked most of it, but something else rang over the undercurrents.

About the Author

Dan Paul grew up in Lake
Wobegon, fishing, playing sports,
and building houses. After
attending the University of
Wisconsin, Madison, and working
at the linear fusion reactor lab,
he explored alternatives to the
dominant codes. While staying in

coops, communes, and squats around the country, he learned
the fundamentals of setting up and operating progressive,
radical, and sustainable alternatives to the codes of
corporations and nations.

Also by Dan Paul

Philosophy of Action Design and Multiplicity by Dan Paul

Book 1 Auto Free Design

Book 2 Workers Health Handbook

Book 3 Save Your Life Prevent Hospital Use

Book 4 Coop Owners Handbook

Book 5 Eye on AI Meeting Needs Sustainably

Book 6 Travels on the Nomadic Terrain

Book 7 Tales of the Urban Shaman

Book 8 Housing in the Danger Zone

Book 9 Corona Time

Book 10 Philosophy of Design, Action and Multiplicity

Coming soon

Landlords Against Eviction

Auto Free USA

Websites

https://viaradmedia.org

https://autofreedesign.com

http://workershealthhandbook.com

http://sylphu.com